A Time For Change

by Alicia Klepeis

Rourke
Educational Media
rourkeeducationalmedia.com

www.rourkeeducationalmedia.com

Edited by: Keli Sipperley
Cover layout by: Rhea Magaro
Interior layout by: Jen Thomas
Cover Illustration by: Laura Tolton

Library of Congress PCN Data

A Time for Change / Alicia Klepeis
 (History Files)
 ISBN (hard cover)(alk. paper) 978-1-68191-676-7
 ISBN (soft cover) 978-1-68191-777-1
 ISBN (e-Book) 978-1-68191-877-8
 Library of Congress Control Number: 2016932449

Printed in the United States of America,
North Mankato, Minnesota

Dear Parents and Teachers,

The History Files series takes readers into significant eras in United States history, allowing them to walk in the shoes of characters living in the periods they've learned about in the classroom. From the journey to a new beginning on the Mayflower, to the strife of the Vietnam War and beyond, each title in this series delves into the experiences of diverse characters struggling with the conflicts of their time.

Each book includes a comprehensive summary of the era, along with background information on the real people that the fictional characters mention or encounter in the novel. Additional websites to visit and an interview with the author are also included.

In addition, each title is supplemented with online teacher/parent notes with ideas for incorporating the book into a lesson plan. These notes include subject matter, background information, inspiration for maker space activities, comprehension questions, and additional online resources. Notes are available at: www.RourkeEducationalMedia.com.

We hope you enjoy the History Files books as much as we do.

Happy reading,
Rourke Educational Media

Table of Contents

Chapter One
Candy and Complaints

• •

Brrrring! Brrrring! As the final bell of the day blared through the Charles Taylor High School, Amari Johnson jumped.

"You jump every day, Amari! You'd think you'd just seen a ghost," her best friend Jackie teased.

"I know. It's crazy, isn't it? I've been at this school since September and I'm still like a jumping bean." Amari grabbed her stack of books and notebooks and headed down the hall to her locker. She filled her leather school bag with all the things she needed for the night's homework. Then she and Jackie headed into the chilly January air.

Walking down Morton Street, Amari and Jackie had their favorite, blowing-off-steam-after-school routines. They always spied on the boys playing handball at the court in

Dorchester Park. Amari tried to stifle a giggle when she saw Marcus Coleman on the court. She'd had a crush on him since the fifth grade when he moved to Mattapan from Virginia. She loved his accent, the way he seemed to linger over every syllable with that southern drawl. And when Marcus played "Mack the Knife" on his acoustic guitar in last year's talent show, she was completely won over. Cute and talented–some people had it all.

After they passed the court, the girls stopped in at Parker's Corner Store.

"Good afternoon, girls. Are you here for a candy run?" Mr. Parker, the elderly shop owner, winked at Amari and Jackie. They used their allowance and babysitting money to buy a treat nearly every day after school.

"Yes, sir." Amari got a few Necco Mint Julep taffies and a pack of Red Vines licorice. Jackie went with her favorite treat, the sweet and chewy Bit-O-Honey bar. Digging nickels and dimes from their change purses, the girls paid Mr. Parker and headed toward Amari's house. Jackie was never in a huge hurry to go home. Her mom was a maid for a rich white family in Milton and usually didn't get home until after dinnertime.

Walking the twelve blocks from Mr. Parker's shop to the Johnson house never seemed to take very long. Jackie and Amari could talk nonstop for hours, especially after being practically silent all day at school. They'd been the best of friends since their kindergarten days.

"Did you see how half the pages of my science book fell out today?" Amari asked Jackie. "These books must be twenty years old. I honestly have no idea how I'm going to keep this pathetic old thing together until the end of the school year."

"I know," Jackie said. "The same thing happened to my math book last year. That's because most of our textbooks are hand-me-downs from wealthier towns or la-di-da neighborhoods in Boston. By the time we get them, the books have already been deemed 'junk' so they get passed along to inner city schools like ours. Sometimes the books are so old that information is out of date."

"Does that happen at Isaiah's school?" Amari wondered.

"Never," Jackie replied. "If you are smart enough to get into Boston Latin—"

"*And* a boy," Amari interrupted.

"Yeah, yeah, and a boy," Jackie continued. "Like I was saying, if you get into Boston Latin, then you get books in fabulous condition and excellent teachers. My brother says the science labs there are amazing. He wants to be a marine biologist when he grows up."

Jackie's older brother Isaiah was sixteen, two years older than Amari and Jackie. But they were all excellent students and took whatever advanced classes they could. Amari often got end-of-the-year awards for her hard work and good grades.

Amari was unusually quiet for a minute. Her forehead was crinkled and her eyes seemed to be looking in the distance. Jackie knew better than to interrupt her friend's thoughts. Finally, Amari asked, "Do you think it would be better to stay at a school like ours or be one of the Little Rock Nine?"

"Wow, girl, where do you come up with this stuff? I was just munching on my Bit-O-Honey and your brain is in full-speed-ahead mode. Let me think out loud … The books and supplies at Central High School in Little Rock are probably heaps nicer than what we have. It *is* a white school, after all. But nobody hates us at Charles Taylor. Well, maybe that nasty girl Kishana. But she doesn't like anyone. Nobody gets in our way when we walk into the building. We don't need the National Guard to protect us."

Amari agreed. "Yeah, I think you're right, Jacks. Remember how white kids ripped at Elizabeth Eckford's clothes? They even clawed at her skin–like animals. It was horrible. All nine of those kids had a rough time at Central High. I don't know if I could have kept going day after day when I knew no one wanted me there."

"Me, neither. Do you think schools in Boston will become integrated soon, Amari?"

"I guess at some point. But after what's happened in Little Rock, I doubt the people in charge are in a big hurry for what you know will be trouble. Did I tell you about my cousin Ronna, one of my Auntie Laila's kids? She was fed up with the crummy supplies at her school. So she started a letter-writing campaign to ask for equal funding for white and black schools. Dozens of her classmates wrote letters and they mailed them to the governor's office."

Jackie was fascinated. "And what happened? Did Ronna hear back?"

"Not yet but it's only been a few weeks from what my dad tells me."

"Maybe we should try it," Jackie suggested.

When Amari opened the front door to her house, a waft of sweet-smelling air enveloped her and Jackie. Something yummy must have just come out of the oven. Mrs. Johnson loved to bake.

After eating some apple crisp, Amari headed to her room. She and Jackie flipped through a few of Mrs. Johnson's *Ebony* magazines. They loved to look through the advertisements and try to recreate the hairstyles on each other. Jackie's short hair was perfect for lots of the cute styles in the magazine. And Amari's was long enough to try the new bouffant style or mini-braids.

They dug through Amari's bureau drawers to see if any of her clothes looked like the ones in the current month's issue. On this particular afternoon, one of her lime green tops was a dead ringer for the one worn by a model in a soda pop ad. Amari's tall, thin frame was perfect for pretending to be a model. Jackie liked to be the stylist and get her friend all decked out in the latest fashions. Mrs. Johnson even loaned a silky scarf and some melamine earrings for the occasion. The girls were nearly done with their make-believe photo shoot when Mrs. Johnson knocked on the door.

"Twenty minutes to dinner," she announced. "By the way girls, you look amazing! If I didn't know better, I'd say you were *Ebony* models." Mrs. Johnson was always one of the most stylish dressers around. Amari loved looking through the photographs of when her mom and dad were first married. They looked dashing on their dates. They loved going to hear live music, especially jazz, and seeing theater productions.

Usually after school Amari and Jackie danced and sang. So in the last remaining minutes before dinner, they dashed to the bin of records in Amari's older sister Tamara's bedroom. Since she was at college, Tamara wouldn't know if her younger sister played her albums, as long as Amari didn't scratch them. Jackie chose one of her all-time favorite tunes, Bobby Day's "Rockin Robin." She put the needle down carefully on the vinyl record. Then the girls let loose with their best, I-don't-care-who-sees-me dance moves. They didn't dare jump or the record might skip and get scratched. Amari erupted into fits of laughter at Jackie's hilarious dance moves. It was a good end to their afternoon.

Chapter Two
Big Doings in Greensboro

· ·

Even though Amari usually despised eating in the school cafeteria, the next day's lunch was different. It still smelled like ancient meatloaf and revolting, metallic canned green beans. But never mind that for the moment … she and Jackie were excited to discuss their idea for a letter-writing campaign with some of their friends.

One of their oldest and closest friends, Denise, shared their enthusiasm for the campaign. "That sounds like something the NAACP Youth Councils might be into. A couple of my cousins in Maryland belong to the junior youth councils. You only have to be twelve to join. And my oldest sister just joined a college unit. She even held picket signs in front of department stores that don't treat black customers fairly."

"Isn't that *all* department stores?" Mable said sarcastically. The other girls at their lunch table started nodding their heads in unison.

"Well, we have to start somewhere, don't we? Otherwise nothing will ever change," Jackie said curtly.

Amari and Jackie were both disappointed in their friends' reactions to their suggestion of writing letters to government officials asking for better funding for black schools. Some of the girls claimed to be worried that they'd get in trouble if Principal Thomas got word of them complaining. Others thought it was a waste of time. Why would white politicians care about their poorly-funded schools, anyway?

After school, Amari and Jackie decided not to let their peers' negativity ruin their enthusiasm. How would things ever change if no one even tried? If Rosa Parks hadn't refused to give up her seat on that Birmingham bus back in 1955, black people would still be giving up their seats to white folks on all those buses. Ms. Parks was willing to go to jail for what she believed in; what she knew was right. Amari thought writing a letter was pretty easy in comparison to being put behind bars. Based on what she'd learned in history class the previous year, free speech was valued in America, right?

Sitting at the red Formica-topped kitchen table in the Johnson house, Jackie and Amari sipped milk and Ovaltine. The girls repeatedly added extra powder, making the chocolaty flavor extra strong. They told Mrs. Johnson about their friends' less-than-excited response to the letter writing campaign. Amari's mother offered some of her best Crane's cream-colored stationery to the girls. "There will always be the naysayers, girls.

People who want to dash your dreams, take your spirits down a peg. I'm proud of you both for doing what you think is right. And despite what your friends said, I actually think that Principal Thomas would be pleased that his students cared enough to try to improve things for others. I'll leave you ladies to it. Good luck!"

After writing lots of drafts on scrap paper, the girls finally decided their letter was ready for the expensive stationery. It read as follows:

February 1, 1960
Governor John Foster Furcolo
Massachusetts State House
Boston, MA 02133

Dear Governor Furcolo,
Good day, Governor. Our names are Amari Johnson and Jackie Harris. We are both

ninth-grade students at Charles Taylor High School, located in Mattapan. We are writing to tell you about what is happening at our school. Both of us have old textbooks that came from wealthier school districts. These books are literally falling apart. Our science books are so out of date that they even have information that is inaccurate. Jackie's older brother attends Boston Latin School. His textbooks are always in beautiful, like-new condition. And the science labs in his school are state-of-the art while many of our Bunsen burners don't function properly and we are always short of the chemicals needed for our experiments.

Why is it that black schools like ours are poorly funded but white schools have excellent resources? Jackie is a great art student but our school never has enough paints, pastels, studio easels, and other materials. In our humble opinions, this does *not seem fair. We get good grades and work hard. Don't we deserve the same educational opportunities as white students?*

It will be a wonderful day when all schools in Massachusetts, whether black or white, have adequate resources. Please help to make our dream for a better school in Mattapan become a reality. Thank you for your time and cooperation.

Sincerely,
Amari Johnson and Jackie Harris

When the girls finished writing their letter, they showed it to Mrs. Johnson. Her eyes welled up a bit. "Wow, girls, this is beautifully written both in terms of content and penmanship. I will bring it to the post office first thing tomorrow, but I'd love to show it to your father before we seal it in the envelope."

"Thanks, Mrs. Johnson," Jackie said. "Amari, I'd better head home soon. I promised my mother I'd start getting dinner ready since it's poker night at the Waldorf house. My mom always has to stay late to get the food and drinks ready for their well-heeled friends."

"Okay, Jacks. Thanks for doing this with me. I feel really good about it."

"Me, too." Jackie smiled. "See you tomorrow."

While Mrs. Johnson was making dinner, Amari flipped on the TV. She needed a distraction from the highly tempting smells coming from the kitchen. Despite her after school snack, she was starving. Perhaps her father was correct in his guess that she was not finished growing yet. Anyway, the smell of pineapple upside down cake was killing her. But, after just a couple of minutes of wondering if she could make it until dinner, her attention shifted to the biggest news story of the night. The news anchor reported that four students from North Carolina Agricultural & Technical College had staged a sit-in at the segregated lunch counter at the Woolworth's department store in Greensboro, North Carolina.

Amari wished her dad were home so he could see the footage. The date was February 1, 1960. All four of these students were black. Their names were Joseph McNeil, Franklin McCain, David Richmond, and Ezell Blair. They sat down at the "whites-only" lunch counter and asked for donuts and coffee. Not surprisingly, they were denied service. But what was surprising was that these four students refused to leave. They read their textbooks and stayed until the store closed for the night. Amari watched the whole news segment, riveted. These young men were about the same age as her big sister, Tamara.

Over dinner that night, Amari had lots to say and many questions to ask. She told her parents all about the news report. Her dad said, "Good for those young men. Black and proud. Sit-ins are a great way to get the message across that black people won't stand for second-class citizen treatment anymore."

"Didn't people have successful sit-ins at other lunch counters before this one?" Amari asked.

"Yes indeed. One that I especially remember took place in Wichita, Kansas, back in 1958. Carol Parks and her cousin Ron Walters were leaders in their local NAACP Youth Council. They organized a sit-in at the Dockum Drugstore, which was a popular place to eat with a soda fountain. Over the course of a few weeks, other students joined in the sit-in, requesting to be served but then denied. Almost a month into the sit-in, the owner decided he was losing too much money by not serving black folks. So, things changed. Carol, Ron, and the other students who participated in the sit-in won a victory for all black people wanting food at Dockum Drugstore, without using violence. And there have been other examples in different locations in the U.S. as well." Dr. Johnson looked pleased for a moment. Then, his expression changed. "But there is much progress that remains to be made. Your momma told me about your letter today. Nice work, Amari."

"Thanks, Dad. Some of my classmates were not very enthusiastic about the letter-writing idea. They said no white politicians care about black schools. I disagree." Amari paused for a second then added, "Do you think *I* could be a part of history like those students in Greensboro who were on the news tonight?"

"Absolutely. Writing the kind of letter you

did today is a way of making history. And as you get older, you may pave the way for other black people in a variety of ways. Your sister is very active in the Youth Council at Howard University. And she hopes to be one of the first black female cardiologists one day." Amari's dad looked proud as he spoke about his eldest daughter.

"Dad, if the Woolworth's lunch counter in Greensboro ever becomes integrated, can we go?"

"You bet, baby. I will take you there for a hamburger and a milkshake as soon as that happens. Deal?"

"Deal."

Chapter Three

Dad's News and Slamming Doors

• •

Like all high school students, Amari always looked forward to Fridays. But they were her favorite day of the week for more reasons than just being the end of the school week. For one thing, she could procrastinate without guilt on her massive piles of homework since there were two extra days to complete her assignments.

Occasionally on Fridays she and Jackie went shopping in Mattapan Square's wacky mix of stores. They usually had to window shop at Grant's Department Store because they didn't have enough money to buy anything. But a few months ago, Amari had brought the birthday money from her grandmother and aunts and bought herself a lime green and yellow dress with cap sleeves.

That day, she'd felt as rich as the white ladies as she carried her shopping bag home. She wore that dress to church many Sundays with her favorite patent leather shoes her mom had bought her at Grant's.

On this Friday afternoon, Jackie needed to go to Kresge's Five and Dime to pick up some Prell shampoo for her mother. Jackie loved the way it smelled but Amari was fond of its bright green color. Jackie also added a fuchsia Maybelline lipstick to her shopping basket.

Amari raised her eyebrows at Jackie. "Who's that for, Jacks?"

"Me, silly. I'm fourteen and a half. I like this color and I have enough money from babysitting those dreadful Williams kids last weekend." Jackie's eyes crinkled at the edges and she was trying hard not to grin like the Cheshire cat. Jackie was obsessed with her mother's beauty products and couldn't wait to wear makeup herself.

"It is a nice color for sure but I thought your mother said you had to be sixteen." Amari was a stickler for details, much to Jackie's chagrin at the moment. Amari couldn't wait to get her own beauty products either but worried she'd get caught if she ever brought some home without permission.

"Yeah, well, I can always play around a little when she's not home, right?" Jackie's smile faded a bit. She'd been excited about buying the lipstick, even if it was against her mom's rules. Amari felt a little badly that she'd blurted out what she was thinking. Maybe she was feeling jealous.

As they walked out of Kresge's, the wind was picking up, blowing the snow all over the sidewalks. It looked as if they were trapped in a snow globe. Neither of the girls wanted to walk any farther than necessary. Since Mattapan Square was about the same distance from each girl's house, the girls each headed their own way after Jackie made her purchases. "See you on Monday, Jacks."

"Bye, Amari. Have a good weekend." Jackie quickly crossed the street and started making her way home.

Fifteen minutes later, Amari dumped her bookbag in her room and changed out of her school clothes. She was excited about "Fun Friday." Every Friday night, the tradition was for Amari and her mother to take the trolley into downtown Boston to meet Amari's dad after work. They had several favorite places to have dinner, depending on the weather and what kind of food they were craving. Amari was trying to guess which restaurant they would select that evening. Ten minutes before she and her mom were supposed to catch the trolley into town, the phone rang.

"Who was that on the phone, Mom?"

"It was your father, baby. He says to stay home tonight because he has some news."

"Did he say what news?" Amari's curiosity was piqued. Dad loved their Fun Friday tradition.

"No. I guess we'll just have to wait and see."

About half an hour later, Dr. Johnson came through the door. He kissed Mrs. Johnson softly on the forehead. "Hello, beautiful. I'm sorry if I fouled up the Friday night plans."

Amari's mom looked nervous. "It's okay, Lamar, but I didn't have time to make a proper meal. I can make something quick, like breakfast for dinner."

"Can we get takeout, pretty please?" Amari suggested, batting her long eyelashes at her parents.

"Great idea, love … Sandra, Amari and I will go get some takeout and bring it home.

Don't stress about it. I was the one who changed the plans." Dr. Johnson quickly changed out of his suit into casual clothes. Then he and Amari headed out.

Walking along the snow-dusted Mattapan streets, Amari tried to encourage her father to share his Fun Friday-breaking news. But he wouldn't budge, teasing her that she would need all her mental energy to make a food decision. Amari smiled at that. She loved getting takeout since it was a rare treat. Mrs. Johnson was a terrific cook who believed that ordering out was not as good as a home-cooked meal. Which was probably true.

Passing by Walker's Restaurant, she was very tempted to get fried chicken, biscuits, and buttermilk mashed potatoes. Then she thought about stopping in the local delicatessen and getting roast beef subs and coleslaw. But after much deliberation, she finally settled on Chinese food. The pork fried rice, chicken strips, and chop suey at China Pearl smelled incredible. She and her dad waited at a little plastic table for the fifteen minutes while the food cooked since it was too blustery to walk around the block without freezing solid. They played Hangman on paper napkins to pass the time. Amari walked at an extra fast pace on the last few blocks, partly so that the food didn't lose all its heat before they got it home.

Outside of Linda Mae's Bakery, Amari put in one last request. "Can we surprise Mom with a cherry pie from here, Dad?" She knew her mom was a huge fan of Linda Mae's desserts but never bought them for herself.

"That's a nice idea, Amari. Why not?" They dashed into the shop and grabbed the very last cherry pie just before Linda Mae switched the sign on the bakery door to read "Closed."

Initially, there was very little conversation among the Johnson family around the dinner table. Just the happy sighs of contented eaters thoroughly enjoying their food. After the main course was consumed, Amari's dad raised his water glass and clinked it with a spoon like they sometimes did at wedding receptions. "Attention, ladies. I have an announcement to make. I have just received word that Shaw University's medical school has offered me a job."

Mrs. Johnson gasped. "Really, Lamar? Wow! That's some news indeed. Congratulations!" She quietly dished each of them up a generous slice of Linda Mae's luscious-looking pie.

Amari looked like a squirrel trying to decide if it should run back to the sidewalk or rush to beat the car heading toward it. "What? I'm confused. I didn't know you applied for a new job, Daddy. Is Shaw in Boston? I haven't heard of it before."

Amari's parents glanced at each other. "Not exactly, love," her dad said. "Shaw is in Raleigh, North Carolina."

"What? North Carolina? When did you apply for this job, Dad?" Amari was seriously flustered. Her voice got louder, her pitch, higher. "You're not going to take that job, are you, Dad? I thought you hated the racism when you were growing up in Georgia. You couldn't wait to move North. Every time we ever go to visit your sisters, you complain about the 'Colored Only' signs and all the Jim Crow laws."

"Amari, don't disrespect your father. This is not your decision," her mother gently chided.

Dr. Johnson took off his glasses and put them gently on the dining room table. He rubbed his fingers over his eyes for a moment before speaking. "I understand that this must come as a shock to you, Amari. But I did not think it made sense to tell you about a job that I might or might not get before a decision was made. Hear me out for a minute, please. Shaw University has a very prestigious medical school. This position would allow me to educate the next generation of black doctors. We need more well-trained doctors, especially in the South. Also, you know your Grandma Rose is getting older and becoming more and more frail. This new job would bring us closer to extended family. I know your mother misses her sisters in South Carolina as well."

Amari picked at her pie, certain that there was steam coming out of her ears. "I have lived my whole life in Mattapan and all my friends are here. Every time we go South in the summer, it's so hot and sticky. I hate the stupid segregated parks, pools, movie theaters, everything. Tamara got to live here

until she went to college! I'm not leaving!"
she bellowed. She sprinted up the stairs and
slammed her bedroom door.

Chapter Four
Goodbye, Boston

• •

Amari never did finish her cherry pie that night. And after that eventful dinner, there were many nights when she sobbed silently into her pillow before drifting off. But gradually, over the month and a half following her dad's big news, Amari adjusted to the fact that she really was leaving Mattapan. On a number of occasions, Mrs. Johnson reminded her daughter that her name, Amari, came from the Yoruba word meaning "strength."

Since there was absolutely nothing she could do to escape the impending move, Amari decided she'd best make the most of her time with Jackie and her family in Boston. In her trusted journal, Amari made a long and detailed list of all the things she hoped to accomplish and see before moving.

One night after their Friday Fun ritual, Amari and her parents went to the Museum of Science. Amari loved sitting with her neck craned to see the myriad stars overhead in the planetarium. She listened to the Sky Talk intently, finding out what stars were going to be bright in the sky that evening. And despite the fact that it was mostly little kids at the Spooky the Owl program, Amari didn't mind sitting cross-legged on the museum floor to hear all about the different kinds of owls. Sometimes, she thought that being an ornithologist would be a really neat job, especially if you got to travel the world looking for exotic bird species.

The last couple of days before the move were strange. Dr. Johnson did not go to work at the hospital. He scheduled vacation days so that he could spend a little time with Amari before his new job started at Shaw. She thought that was really sweet of him, especially since she knew she'd been so moody and irritable these last few weeks.

The Saturday before the move, Amari and her father spent the whole day together, which was a rare treat. Mrs. Johnson was still packing up her best dishes and appliances in the kitchen and boxing up all of their clothes. Amari and her dad went out to breakfast and ordered blueberry pancakes slathered with butter and pure maple syrup. He even let her order a real, caffeine-laden cup of coffee just like he did, something her mother would never have agreed to. Amari had been sipping her dad's coffee ever since she was a toddler. There was just something about its rich smell and holding the warm mug that she found both comforting and grown-up.

"What's your pleasure, young lady? I am happy to go wherever you'd like today. It's beautiful out; the sun is shining and the fine city of Boston awaits," her dad said.

"Could we walk along some sections of the Freedom Trail today? I like investigating all the old buildings and finding out what happened there. We could wander through Boston Common one more time and then go to the North End to get some of those Italian cookies and cannolis at Mike's Pastry. If it stays nice out, we could eat the treats outside somewhere in a little park. What do you think?" Amari grinned broadly at her father, pleased with the plan she'd dreamed up weeks ago in her journal.

"That sounds like the perfect day, baby. I think you have given some serious thought to your last adventures in the city. I am impressed." Dr. Johnson took his daughter's hand. "Let me pay the bill and then we'll be off, free as the breeze."

The day went exactly as Amari had planned. She and her dad enjoyed looking in old bookstores, buying warm spiced pecans and walnuts from a street vendor, and reading historical plaques in various churches and graveyards across Boston. The only thing that didn't go perfectly was that Mike's Pastry was sold out of cannolis. So Amari settled on a cup of pistachio gelato instead. She also remembered to buy a little rum cake for her mom since that was her absolute favorite dessert in the world.

The night before the move, Amari had Jackie over for a farewell dinner of baked macaroni-and-cheese. Mrs. Johnson took several photographs of the girls with the family's new Nikon camera. Photography was a hobby of hers. Jackie presented Amari with a sketch of the two of them that she'd made for Amari's new bedroom in Raleigh. She got teary when she handed it to her best friend. "I'm going to miss you so much, Amari. School is going to be so weird without you there. Promise me you will write?" Jackie hugged Amari like perhaps Amari couldn't move away if she didn't let go of her.

Amari also cried. "Of course I'll write, Jacks. You know I love writing. And maybe your mom will let you come visit for a week during summer vacation." Dr. Johnson and Amari walked Jackie home after dinner. The girls exchanged one last hug and then Jackie walked up the steps to her apartment, trying to control her fast-flowing tears.

Early the next morning, the moving truck arrived. Four huge men made dozens of trips in and out of Amari's house, carrying heavy furniture around as if it weighed nothing. In less than four hours, everything was in the truck. The only house that Amari could ever remember living in was empty. It seemed so strange. But there was no time to waste since they needed to be in Raleigh by dinnertime the next night to meet the movers. Amari dreaded the twelve-hour ride. She hated being confined for so long, though she was a bit curious about what she'd see along the way.

"Goodbye, house," Amari said quietly. She hopped into the back seat of the car with her trusty old pink teddy bear, Rosie. Her Aunt Melanie had given Rosie to Amari for her first birthday. Amari's dad put his maps on the front seat. Her mother put on her sunglasses and the three of them were off, heading for Route 95 South.

The first few hours flew by, partly because Amari fell asleep not too far into the ride, probably somewhere in Rhode Island. All of the packing, last outings in Boston, and goodbyes had left her feeling emotionally drained and physically exhausted. When she woke up, Amari heard her parents talking logistics. She looked out the window, trying to thaw out. "Can we take a bathroom stop soon?" she asked.

"Sure, baby, I'll keep my eyes open for a rest stop. My legs could use a stretch anyway," Dr. Johnson said. They pulled into a parking lot just over the New Jersey border. Amari was furious when she noticed the "Colored Only" signs at the water fountains and restrooms. She would have boycotted the facilities but she really had to go. The ladies' room was downright filthy.

Back in the car, Amari complained about the rest stop. "I'll bet the white bathroom was so much cleaner than ours. And I would never want to drink from that fountain for black folks. It looked like no one had wiped it down in ages. Yuck!" she griped. Her parents acknowledged her complaints but Mrs. Johnson said that she wanted to try to stay positive on the ride. Amari's dad suggested that they play some kind of game. He was an avid game player–Scrabble, Monopoly, checkers, you name it.

Even though she wasn't really in the mood to start, Amari agreed to try her dad's idea. First they played I Spy. Then they played the license plate game. Amari was quite pleased with herself when she saw an Alaska plate and a New Mexico plate. Finally, they went with Amari's favorite activity in the car where one person starts a story and each person tells a sentence in succession. The three Johnsons came up with a great travel tale about a man named Felix who opened the world's biggest candy shop on an island in the Indian Ocean.

Just outside of Baltimore, Amari started getting fidgety so they decided to call it a night. They pulled into the parking lot of the Greendale Motor Lodge. Dr. Johnson left Amari and her mom in the car. He went in and asked for a room and was refused service because he was black. So he headed down the road to the next motel. The same thing happened again. Dr. Johnson tried to remain calm but Amari could see his growing agitation. "How many years of medical school have I gone through? I have saved how many people's lives in a major hospital in Boston? Am I still not good enough to stay here? Is my cash less valuable than a white man's money?" Mrs. Johnson and Amari kept quiet, knowing he needed to vent for a minute.

Finally, after three refusals, the Johnsons found a place that offered accommodations to black people. They dropped off their bags and took the motel owner's suggestion for a good nearby restaurant within walking distance. Amari decided that some music from the jukebox might be just the ticket to shake off the bad mood. She asked her mother for a few dimes. The Seeburg Select-o-matic whirred into action. Amari got back to the booth just as the first song came on. While waiting for their food to arrive, Amari danced at the table to "Shimmy, Shimmy, Ko-Ko Pop" by Little

Anthony and the Imperials and "Wild One" by Bobby Rydell. Her mom even got into the spirit, tapping her feet to "Baby (You've Got What It Takes)" by Dinah Washington and Brook Benton. The fun vibes of the music cheered all of them up.

Amari crawled into bed in her favorite lilac nightgown. Her mother kissed her forehead saying, "Tomorrow we'll be in our new house. And since the kids are on school vacation this week, you'll have a whole week to settle in before you start your new school." Amari had trouble falling asleep. She wondered what her new school would be like and how different it would be to live in North Carolina. Her stomach was full of butterflies. Not just those little yellow ones. More like the giant ones you see in pictures of the rainforests.

Chapter Five
New House, Strange Vibes

• •

Amari had several weird dreams that night. She dreamed about mean girls dumping milk on her in the school cafeteria. She dreamed that her hair all broke off because her mom had left the relaxing chemicals on too long and that she had to go to school practically bald. She dreamed that she had an older brother who was in the same high school she attended. By the time morning rolled around, Amari felt like she had gone through a million adventures in real life. She was wiped out.

The last five hours of the drive to Raleigh flew by. Amari enjoyed seeing Lake Anna and the James River out her window. There were more "Colored Only" signs at the rest stop in Virginia. But Amari told herself that perhaps her mother had had the right idea last night—

she should just focus on the positive. There was certainly no sense in getting mad every time you had to stop to use the bathroom.

As they approached the city of Raleigh, Mrs. Johnson was navigating since she was an excellent map reader. Amari's dad exited the highway. Winding their way through downtown Raleigh, Amari rolled down her window. She loved the sun on her face and enjoyed how the breeze felt much warmer than it had back in Boston. After a few minutes, she noticed a sign that said Battery Heights. "Isn't that where our house is?" Amari asked her mother.

"Good eyes, Amari. You're right. We must be getting really close," Mrs. Johnson replied. "Lamar, take the second left onto Miller Street."

Amari turned her head quickly from side to side, as if she were watching a tennis match between Rod Laver and Alex Olmedo.

She tried to take in everything–what kind of flowers people planted, where the mailboxes were, the colors of the houses, and so on. With no double or triple-decker apartment buildings, the neighborhood definitely felt less urban than where she'd lived in Mattapan. All of the houses in Battery Heights were set back from the street. The majority of them looked to be only one-story high, which was also very different. She didn't see any little corner stores like Parker's back home. Amari wondered where a black girl like herself would go if she had money for a candy bar or a snack with friends. *If I ever make any here,* she thought.

Amari was shaken from all the thoughts floating around her head when her mother announced, "We're here. This is it."

Her father pulled into the concrete driveway. "What do you think, Amari Jane?"

"Wow, it's nice!" Amari replied. "The

neighborhood seems modern and kind of fancy. How many houses did you and Mom visit that weekend I stayed at Jackie's?"

"About seven or eight, I think," her mom said. "This one is very light inside. I know how you and your dad don't like dark rooms. The real estate agent told us that the people in Battery Heights have an active social life with pool and tennis parties and neighborhood get-togethers at the holidays. Apparently there are a number of kids living here, too."

"That sounds great. Can I go explore the house?" Amari was excited to see what the inside looked like.

"Of course," her dad said. "Let me just find the key in the envelope I have here."

Amari walked in and dashed from one room to the next. The house had three decent-sized bedrooms; a kitchen with a little breakfast nook; a formal dining room; a simple bathroom with pink tiles and a matching toilet; and a spacious living room. All of the rooms had windows, but the living room window was divided into three separate sections that opened out and overlooked the front garden. Whoever had lived in this house before them must have had a green thumb. And the magnolia tree was just starting to bud.

Amari was dying to figure out which bedroom was hers. Her dad said she could choose either of the smaller two bedrooms since Tamara wouldn't care. After all, she lived at college most of the year anyway. Amari chose the room at the far end of the house. It was painted light green and had two windows, one of which had several trees close by. Her room even had a little closet. Her old room in Boston had a small built-in storage cabinet, but no closet.

Amari's mom had told her on the car ride that their house in Raleigh was only built a couple of years earlier so everything was in good shape. Unlike Mattapan, which had been inhabited for a long time, the Battery Heights subdivision started developing around 1956. That's why it seemed more modern than her old neighborhood.

Amari and her parents brought in the few bags they had in the car. Amari was keen on exploring the nooks and crannies of the yard and walking around the neighborhood. Unfortunately, her father had other plans. "I know we just got here, Amari, and that you've been in the car a lot. But the movers are due here in a couple of hours. Since tomorrow is Sunday and the grocery store will be closed, I'm thinking we should get at least a little food for the weekend. Then you and your mother can do a bigger shop when I go to work on Monday."

"Rats! I really wanted to stay here." Her dad raised his eyebrows at her. "Yes sir, I'm coming," she said. They found an A&P Market not too far away and got a few bags of groceries. Amari found it strange that practically everyone in the store was black. She didn't see any white folks in the store and didn't hear anyone speaking languages besides English, which definitely was different from Mattapan's markets.

The movers arrived later than expected so it was dark out when they showed up. By the time they left, it was nearly ten o'clock. Amari was disappointed that she couldn't sleep in her own bed. But since she found some of her blankets in a well-labeled box, she decided to crash on the carpeted floor of her new room.

On Monday morning, Amari's dad was up and out of the house super early. She guessed he was nervous about traffic and getting to work on time. She sat in the sunny breakfast nook eating a bowl of Corn Flakes. "Mom, can we go to town today? I'd like to get a few things to decorate my new room, like maybe a bulletin board and a frame to hang up Jackie's sketch of us."

"I don't see why not. I have some errands to do myself. The shops will be closed by the time Dad gets back from work with the car. Put on a nice dress, please."

"How come? I thought we were just doing errands," Amari said.

"Let's just say I have a feeling about what it might be like in Raleigh, okay?"

Amari changed into her long yellow dress and put a matching ribbon in her hair. She wore her favorite pearl earrings. Her mom looked beautiful, as always, but a little unsettled. Amari decided not to ask about it. The two of them waited at the bus stop. About ten minutes later, the Raleigh City Coach Line bus pulled up. After paying her fare, Amari started walking down the bus aisle. The white folks were all sitting up front and stared at her as she walked by. She tried to avoid making eye contact with them and kept walking until she was near the back door of the bus. Some black folks stared at her while others just looked out the window or down at the floor. She slid into a seat, feeling strange and out of place. Her mother did not chat as she often did on the trolley in Boston. Instead, she just stared at her purse. Eventually, the driver announced, "Downtown Raleigh. Last stop for this bus."

Amari wanted to walk along a couple of the downtown streets before deciding where to shop. In front of Kress, Hudson-Belk, and Woolworth's were signs. One said "Luncheonette Temporarily Closed." Another said "Closed in the Interest of Public Safety." The third said "We Reserve the Right to Serve the Public as We See Fit." She asked her mom about the signs.

Mrs. Johnson looked disappointed. "Some businesses would rather close their lunch counters and lose money than serve people like you and me. Students from Shaw and St. Augustine have been busy protesting here in Raleigh over the segregated facilities. What is going on in Greensboro is happening here too."

Amari nodded. "I'm glad. I heard on the radio that the Ambassador Theatre still has separate entrances for black and white people. Tamara can see a first-run movie in Washington, D.C., and sit where she likes. There's nothing wrong with us."

"I agree, love. I tell you what. Let's buy the paper while we are in town and you can find out more about what's happening here in Raleigh. In the meantime, we should get some decorations for your room and pick up your school supplies."

Amari had to look through the goods in three different stores to find everything on her list. And in each shop, white workers watched her as she gathered her items. They looked at her like they thought she was going to steal their merchandise. She did not like the way that made her feel.

All week Amari and her mom got acquainted with Raleigh and Battery Heights. One of their new neighbors brought over a peach pie. Another dropped off a basket of biscuits and gravy. Amari had seen some kids at a distance but none of them looked to be quite her age. But there might be some chances for her to babysit, by the look of things.

The evening before the first day at her new school, Amari spent loads of time trying to decide what to wear. She finally decided on a sweater and skirt set she'd gotten just before leaving Boston. That night she also had her mom straighten her hair. She hated the smell of the hair relaxers. They stung her eyes and stunk up the house. But she was not going to start school without her hair looking as smooth as she could get it. She had no idea what was in fashion down in Raleigh. She did not want to stand out in her new high school if she could avoid it.

Chapter Six
After-School Drama

• •

Amari woke up way before her alarm on her first day of school in Raleigh. She could barely bring herself to eat the toast with butter and cinnamon sugar her mother had made for her. "I feel sick to my stomach, Mom. Do I have to go today? Maybe I could just start school in September since there's only one term of the year left anyway," Amari pleaded.

"I know you are feeling incredibly nervous, love. That's perfectly normal. In fact, it would be strange for you to not be worried. But you'll get through the day, one class at a time, just like at Charles Taylor." Mrs. Johnson grabbed Amari's book bag and lunch and walked her down the path to the end of their street. They had done a trial run earlier in the week so Amari would know exactly where she was going. It only took twelve minutes to walk to Battery Heights High School.

Approaching the steps of the school, Amari could feel acid rising in her throat. She knew no one. Not a soul. Every day back home, she and Jackie walked to school—elementary, junior high, and high school—together. Unless Jackie was sick, Amari never had to show up alone. She timidly climbed the stairs, ignoring the many unfamiliar sets of eyes staring at her. The wooden entry doors seemed enormous and heavy as she pulled their handles. Glancing down the main hallway, she saw groups of kids in the distance. Some were tough looking, decked out in boots and leather jackets. But like every high school in America, there were also stunningly beautiful girls chatting by the lockers.

Amari headed for the school's main office since she didn't have her schedule yet. The secretary handed her a piece of paper and told her the number of her homeroom: 312A. Her school in Mattapan had had three floors, which meant it was compact and easy to navigate. Spanning an entire city block, Battery Heights High School seemed mammoth in comparison. Like her new house, it was a ranch style building. Amari guessed that was one way to beat the heat. No school for black kids was going to have air conditioning when the weather got hot.

The first bell rang, making her jump, and suddenly loads of students dashed past her. She was still looking for her classroom but no one stopped to ask if she needed help. The second bell rang. "Darn, I'm late," Amari muttered under her breath. A couple of minutes later, she found 312A. The homeroom teacher, Mrs. James, found Amari an unoccupied seat, then accompanied her to her first period class.

The first four classes all blended together. Each teacher had Amari introduce herself, which was mortifying in her opinion, before giving her a textbook. Amari thought some of the books were in even worse shape than the ones back home, something she would have thought was impossible. But being the new kid, she said nothing. At lunch, Amari sat at a table in the back of the cafeteria, hoping to stay under the radar and not attract attention. She ate her peanut butter sandwich and chocolate chip cookies as fast as she could, staring down at the table. She didn't want to make it even more obvious that she had no friends.

The homework load seemed lighter than in Boston, which was nice. But some classes had more behavior problems—kids shouting out in class instead of raising their hands; others throwing spitballs and passing notes. Amari found it hard to concentrate. When the two o'clock bell rang, Amari could not wait to leave. But she decided to hold back for a couple of minutes before packing up her bag for the night. That way, she figured at least some of the after-school chaos would settle down a bit.

When Amari finally started walking home, the sidewalks looked crowded, full of strangers. So she decided to try an alternative route that might have fewer people on it. A couple of blocks down, a group of white kids stood outside a corner store. She heard some hooting and hollering but didn't think much about it. Then, out of sheer curiosity, Amari quickly glanced to see what the fuss was about. "Hey, girl, what are you doing on our turf?" one boy said. "No black kids getting cream sodas in here. Go back to your part of town!"

Amari immediately looked at the ground and started walking faster. Unfortunately, some of the kids started trailing her. She ran as fast as she could with her heavy school bag on her back but the boys chased her for a couple of blocks. She could feel the leather straps of her bursting-at-the-seams book bag digging into her shoulders, but she didn't dare slow down. Finally, panting and sweating, she turned the corner into her neighborhood, and was alone. She burst through the front door like a hurricane. Tears streamed from her eyes.

"What happened, Amari?" Mrs. Johnson looked stunned. "Why are you crying?"

Amari tried to catch her breath, her chest still heaving from the sprinting. Sobbing, she mumbled, "They … they … chased me home. They said to go back to *my* part of town."

"Who said that? Who chased you, baby?" Amari's mom was livid.

Amari told her mother about her rotten day from start to finish. When she was done, and the tears had stopped, she asked if she could call Jackie.

"Yes, Amari. Just remember it is a long-distance call and expensive so you will have to keep it relatively short, okay?"

Amari felt much better after her conversation with Jackie. She knew she would. Jackie was delighted to hear her best friend's familiar voice and to hear all about Amari's new house and school. She suggested that Amari reach out to some of the quieter kids in her classes. Then maybe she could find people to sit with at lunch and also to walk home with. Before hanging up, Jackie promised to write a letter that weekend and so did Amari.

Amari headed to her bedroom, looking much nicer with the new bulletin board she'd filled with photos of Mattapan, her old house, ribbons from a dance she'd attended, and a colorful bookmark Jackie had painted her the previous year in art class. With her bed covered in a new lilac bedspread, the room seemed cheerful and full of promise. Even if Amari herself wasn't feeling that way.

After doing some math and English homework, Amari clicked on the transistor radio she'd gotten for Christmas. The announcer reported that the sit-ins in Greensboro were still going on. She was fascinated by the interviews of some of the students who had participated in the sit-ins. One said a white man had dumped ketchup on his head while another said white folks had spit at her. Many had racial insults shouted in their faces. And yet they all remained committed to the nonviolent methods of protest.

Amari was stunned at these students' ability to remain calm even in the face of such hostility. The male and female students just waited and waited to be served at the

Woolworth's lunch counter. Some studied at the counter as a way to pass the time productively. But every day they continued their work toward racial equality. As a NAACP representative said, "These young people, tomorrow's leaders, are seeking much more than the opportunity to eat where and as others eat in public places. They seek self-respect, recognition and dignity."

In the next segment of the radio broadcast, Amari heard that Dr. Martin Luther King Jr. would be coming to meet with student activists at Shaw University. She had read heaps of articles in the newspapers about Dr. King's work in cities around the nation. In her elementary school social studies class, Amari studied Dr. King's work with the bus boycott in Montgomery, Alabama. She also saw a television program about the Southern Christian Leadership Conference and their work to get black voters registered in the South.

Amari imagined getting the chance to hear Dr. Martin Luther King Jr. speak. She marveled at what a great public speaker he was. Her mother often talked about how much wonderful work Dr. King was doing for black people all over the United States.

Suddenly, Amari's attention shifted when she heard her father's deep voice in the hallway. "Amari, dinner is ready," he called. She switched off her radio and headed to the dining room.

Over dinner, Amari told her dad about the rough day she'd had at school.

"The first day is is always tough," he said. "It's bound to get better, Amari."

Amari nodded. He was probably right. But she definitely would not make the same mistake of using a different route home. Changing the topic, she begged, "Daddy, do you think we can see Dr. King when he comes to Shaw? You teach there so I'm sure you can go."

Her dad smiled. "Hold up, little lady. I hadn't heard about Dr. King coming to Shaw. Remember I'm in the medical school part of campus and have not finished reading today's newspaper yet." He took his glasses off and looked like he was thinking. "I just started this job, Amari, so don't be too sure about anything. Dr. King is going to be extremely busy with the students. I'll see what I can do but I can't make any promises."

"All right, Daddy. I understand. But I really hope we can see him," she said.

Chapter Seven
An Unbelievable Opportunity

• •

Amari's second day at Battery Heights High School was definitely better than her first. She realized that Jackie was right. She couldn't just expect kids to reach out to her. She needed to introduce herself and show people she was friendly. She wasn't some stuck-up newcomer from Boston.

In math class, Amari met a girl named Grace. They were partners on the day's challenge problem in geometry. Amari joined Grace and her friends at lunch. They asked her lots of questions about life in Boston, her old school, what it was like to be in the North, and so on. Amari told them about her big sister and going to college in Washington, D.C. Grace was the only one at the table whose parents had both gone to college. But Amari didn't pick her friends that way. Jackie's mom was a maid. Lots of her friends' parents had different jobs—hairdresser, construction worker, waitress, et cetera.

Amari told the girls what had happened to her after school the day before. None of them seemed surprised. A girl named Nicole told her, "Yeah, that street you chose to walk along is close to the white part of town. You'd be better off sticking closer to the shops near South Pettigrew Street in the future. Where do you live anyway?"

"Miller Street," Amari said. Amari thought she saw two of the girls raise their eyebrows at each other but that might have just been her imagination. She didn't want people to think that she was some rich doctor's kid. After all, she had to vacuum and scrub floors every weekend to get her allowance, just like most of the other kids she knew back home.

Luckily, it turned out that Stephanie lived a couple of streets over in the same neighborhood. She offered to show Amari some of the shortcuts home and which streets or places she should avoid. After a couple of days of walking home together, Amari asked Stephanie a question that had been bugging her since she arrived in Raleigh. "Are there any nice shopkeepers around who sell candy? I miss getting my Cherry Flipsticks after school."

Stephanie stopped dead in her tracks. "Really? You like Cherry Flipsticks?"

Amari wasn't sure how to respond. After a split second of deliberating with herself, she went with honesty. "Yeah, they're my favorite. Those and Abba-Zaba bars. Why?"

"You are about the only one in Battery Heights who likes them. Other than me, that is." Stephanie looked delighted. They walked a little out of their way and stopped at the Sweet Shack. Stephanie introduced Amari to the owner, Mrs. Pierce. She was a nice lady, probably in her fifties. She wore a colorful apron with candy over her dress.

"Nice to meet you, young lady. I hope we'll be seeing you again," she said.

"You certainly will, ma'am. I love candy!" Heading out from the store, Amari and Stephanie pretended to apply their lipstick-like Cherry Flipsticks to their lips before biting into the taffy. Then they broke out into giggles.

Gradually, each day Amari met new kids at school. She told her parents over dinner one night that making friends reminded her of making popcorn. At first it's just one pop, but then bam—pop, pop, pop. And then you've got lots of kernels, or friends. Amari still missed Mattapan and wrote long, detailed letters each week to Jackie. But she was starting to feel more comfortable in Battery Heights. She even got a babysitting job working for her neighbors, the Jeffersons. They had two adorable toddlers and paid well. Fifty cents an hour!

A few days after Amari shared the news about Dr. King coming to Shaw, her father brought up the topic over dinner. "I know you have probably been wondering about the Dr. King visit at Shaw, Amari. And I have been asking around, despite the fact that I don't know many people here yet. I was directly told that I can't get us in to participate in the student workshops with Dr. King. Given how many college students want to be part of these workshops, I'm not surprised."

Amari sighed. She'd been so sure that her dad could get them in.

"But," her father continued, "one of my colleagues has a brother who is a journalist. Now there is a very good chance that the answer will still be no. So don't get your hopes up."

It turned out that a couple of days later, Dr. Johnson heard back from his colleague. Amari squealed when he told her the news— she would be getting to see Dr. Martin Luther

King Jr. in person! They would have to sit in the back row of his press conference. But Amari was so excited. And so was her dad, truth be told.

Wearing her very best dress and carrying a notebook and pen, Amari sat down in the last row of a very full room. Reporters from newspapers and television stations filled the seats beside and in front of her. When Dr. King entered the room, Amari was blinded for a minute by all of the flashbulbs going off. Then, he began to speak:

"This is an era of offensive on the part of oppressed people. All peoples deprived of dignity are on the march on every continent throughout the world. The student sit-ins movement represents just such an offensive in the history of the Negro people's struggle for freedom. The students have taken the struggle for justice into their own strong hands. In less than two months more Negro freedom fighters have revealed to the nation and the world

their determination and courage than has occurred in many years. They have embraced a philosophy of mass direct nonviolent action ... Today the leaders of the sit-in movement are assembled here from ten states and some forty communities to evaluate the recent sit-ins and to chart future goals. They realize that they must now evolve a strategy for victory."

Amari took notes as fast as her hand would allow. For once, she was grateful to Mr. Thompson, who made her take such speedy notes back in eighth grade science class. She glanced at her father who kept nodding his head in agreement with Dr. King's powerful words.

Dr. King went on to speak about "selective buying" where people should only buy goods from businesses that respect black people. He said that the students needed to train more volunteers who would be willing to go to jail rather than just post bond and go free. The "jail without bail" tactic meant that by refusing to pay money to avoid going to jail, protesters would fill the jails and burden the resources of the state. Amari liked when Dr. King said "The youth must take the freedom struggle into every community in the South without exception."

When Dr. King finished talking, Amari and her dad stood up and clapped. So did several other people in the audience. She clapped until her hands ached. Some of the reporters stayed seated but she was thrilled and inspired by Dr. King's powerful words. She wanted to be part of the freedom struggle. She wanted to work for justice and equality for all people. One reporter came up to Amari. He asked her, "What did you think of the speech, young lady?"

"It was amazing, sir," she replied. "I can't wait until I can be part of the struggle for freedom. But for now, I am hoping to share what I learned today with the students at my school by writing an article for the school newspaper."

The man smiled, "That's a terrific idea!" He looked at Dr. Johnson and said, "You've got a smart young woman here. A budding journalist and a freedom fighter. Well done!" And he headed out to the courtyard where the college students were congregating.

Amari's dad leaned closer to his daughter. "I didn't know you were considering signing up for the school newspaper."

She looked a little embarrassed, "Well, I wasn't really sure if they would take an unknown freshman like me. But I think a first-hand scoop from Dr. Martin Luther King Jr. might give me a little extra credibility, don't you think?"

"I sure do. Now, unfortunately, I'm due back in class in twenty minutes. But your mother should be waiting in my office to take you home. Thanks for coming with me,

Amari. I'm really glad you pushed to go. Dr. King is an incredible speaker. He makes me believe that black people can do anything in this nation of ours."

"Me, too."

On the bus ride home from Shaw University, Amari told her mother all about his speech, what the reporter said to her, and how she was going to try writing for the school newspaper. She also decided that she wanted to pick up her letter-writing campaign where she left off with Jackie. In her notebook, she started a list of all the changes she'd like to see in America. She planned to write letters about getting better facilities in black schools, finding hotels or restaurants that don't turn families like hers away, getting rid of the Jim Crow laws … Amari's list grew and grew.

Chapter Eight
The Ultimate Milkshake

• •

"Great article!" "I can't believe you saw Dr. King in person!" "Loved your piece!" Walking down the hallway, Amari couldn't believe how many students came up to congratulate her. *The Battery Heights High School Gazette* had come out the previous day and, much to her surprise, lots of people had actually read her article. She was so excited. Even juniors and seniors stopped her in the hallway to ask, "Hey, aren't you Amari Johnson?" She felt like a celebrity when just a short time before no one knew who she was.

Mrs. Morgan, the school newspaper advisor, stopped in to see Amari while she was eating her lunch. "Well, young lady, I don't think an article has caused this much buzz in our school paper since ... well, since Rosa Parks refused to give up her seat years ago. I do hope that you will continue writing articles for us. You have the potential to be quite the journalist. Be sure to come to our next meeting after school next Tuesday when we plan the topics for our next issue."

"I ... I'd love to join you," Amari stammered. "Thanks, Mrs. Morgan."

When Mrs. Morgan left the cafeteria, Amari's friends at the lunch table high-fived her. Brianna commented on how she thought Mrs. Morgan was fierce. Anna said she thought Mrs. Morgan was a fashion plate. It was true that she was definitely the most stylish of all the female teachers. Stephanie said she'd heard a rumor that Mrs. Morgan participated in one of the sit-ins in Wichita back when she was a college student.

"I wouldn't be shocked if she did. There's no way she'd be afraid of sitting at a drug store counter," Sarah acknowledged.

The day flew by. Amari was floating on air after all the kind words people had about her article. Over the next few weeks, she became friendly with the school newspaper crowd. Most of them were pretty nice, though some of the editors, especially the seniors, could be gruff on occasion. Amari wrote two articles each week. None of them were on the front page like her Dr. King piece, but she knew better than to expect that. She was only a freshman, after all.

Amari wrote an article about the continuation of the Greensboro sit-ins. She listened to interviews of students who participated on her transistor radio and watched the evening news on television with her father. She gleaned the Raleigh newspaper each night after she finished her homework. Amari also wrote a fascinating piece about the segregation of public swimming pools in America.

Over dinner, she asked her parents, "Did you know that in the mid-1930s black people made up fifteen percent of St. Louis's population? But they only took one-and-a-half percent of the number of swims."

"I did not know that, Amari. Why do you think that was the case?" her father asked.

"People with skin like us only had access to one small indoor pool but white folks in St. Louis could choose from nine different swimming pools. And some were big, resort-style pools. It hardly seems fair. Did the people in charge think black people didn't get hot or what? In some American cities, black teens were badly beaten for trying to access public swimming pools. I read a quote from a white woman who said she didn't want the pool her people swam in to be infected by the communicable diseases black people brought. Isn't that outrageous?" Amari was indignant.

"It sure is outrageous, baby. I'm glad you are bringing up these issues in your school newspaper. You're making your fellow students think. Maybe you could even write some letters to the powers that be about this issue," her mom suggested.

"Good idea, Mom. But first I have to get through my next article."

A few weeks later, Amari and Stephanie were getting their afternoon candy fix at the Sweet Shack. Suddenly, two hands covered Amari's eyes. Amari screamed out loud and started fidgeting like crazy. The hands gradually released their grip. Heart pounding, Amari twirled around. She was expecting to see some bullies or kids from another part of town. She was all fired up to give the person grabbing her a piece of her mind—or a blow from her fist, if necessary. But then she saw her "attacker." It was her big sister, Tamara.

"Tamara!" Amari yelled. "You're home! You nearly gave me a heart attack. How did you know I'd be here?" She hugged her sister tightly.

"Mom told me that you almost always come here after school. I thought I'd surprise you … and I guess I did." Tamara laughed as she mimicked Amari's reaction. "Wanna buy me some Mike and Ikes, sis? I left my purse at home."

"Of course, Tam." Amari paid and introduced Stephanie to her sister. Then Stephanie went to the market on her own to do an errand for her mother. After going their separate ways, Tamara told Amari that she'd taken the early train from Washington that morning and had just made it home. Their dad had picked her up during his lunch break and brought her to the house. The sisters talked about the new house, Battery Heights High School, and their plans for the summer. Tamara said that she was going to be an intern with a cardiologist at the hospital close to Shaw. She would get to shadow the doctor on some days and help with paperwork and other jobs he needed done.

Amari thought it was great to have Tamara home. She hadn't realized how much she missed having her around. Dinner conversations definitely became more lively. One night Tamara talked about going to the non-segregated movie theater in Washington, D.C.

"Is there really such a thing, Tam? What's it like?"

"Well, the Dupont Theater is small. It opened in March 1948 as an art house theater. When you walk in, there is a big lounge, like a modern club room. When you're waiting for the next movie to start, you can order tea and coffee. Doesn't matter if you have dark skin or light skin. My friends and I love to go there. It hardly matters what movie is showing. We give our money to the Dupont because we want to spread the message that all movie theaters should be integrated." Tamara smiled with a faraway look. Amari guessed she was remembering fun nights out with her friends. She hoped that by the time she went to college, all movie theaters would welcome black patrons.

On Saturdays, Amari and Tamara got into the routine of spending the mornings together. During the school week, Amari had homework and newspaper duties keeping her busy and Tamara was gone for her internship until dinnertime every night. With the little money that they both earned, they often enjoyed going out for coffee and donuts or ice cream sundaes. They both had a serious sweet tooth.

One Saturday, Tamara was shopping for a new dress. She was debating between two—a white one with tiny orange flowers and a turquoise one with thin white stripes. "I sure wish I could try these on. It's so hard to decide which one will look better."

Amari sympathized. "Yeah, I know. It drives me crazy that white people can try on clothing before they buy it but we are not allowed. It's not as if we're going to damage the dresses just by touching them."

"No kidding, sis," Tamara said. "And if I had enough money, I could just buy them both and return the one I didn't like as well. But we aren't allowed to do that either. It's ironic how these big department stores are more than happy to take our money but not give us the same privileges as the white ladies shopping here." She put the turquoise dress back on the rack. "No sense ruining our mood right now. Let's pay for this one and then go grab two root beer floats. This hot, sticky weather is making me thirsty."

"Sounds like a plan," Amari agreed. "Where are we going, anyway?"

"My boss told me about a great soda fountain run by one of our neighbors from Battery Heights. He said it's one of the nicest spots for black folks and is very close to the main shops downtown." After a short, sweaty walk, Amari and her sister found themselves sitting at the cool marble counter. The soda fountain looked so inviting. The mirrors behind it were shiny, the stools were bright red, and the lady behind the counter was very sweet.

Over their delicious, cool floats, Tamara gabbed away. She told Amari about the other girls in her dormitory. Her roommate, Rosemary, had a real sense of style and even sewed them matching bedspreads with fabric they picked out together. Most Saturday nights, there was a mixer on campus.

"Are there any cute boys?" Amari asked.

Tamara laughed. "Oh, yes, lots of them. Rosemary met her boyfriend at one of them. His name is Otis and he's a super nice guy. But I have also met some great people at the NAACP Youth Council I joined on campus." Amari said that she'd been wanting to join one too. Tamara suggested that maybe she could share what her group was working on until Amari got hooked up with a local chapter herself.

One late July evening, Amari was sitting on the sofa watching the evening news with her dad while her mother and Tamara were finishing the cooking. The news anchor reported that the Greensboro sit-ins at Woolworth's had finally worked: the lunch counter was now desegregated! Amari and Dr. Johnson whooped and hollered at the exciting news.

"What's going on, Lamar?" Amari's mom raced out of the kitchen to see what was happening. When he told her, she and Tamara added some cheers of their own. Over dinner, Amari reminded her dad of his promise to take her to eat at the Greensboro Woolworth's if it became integrated. Dr. Johnson said he'd take the whole family on his next day off.

True to his word, the four Johnsons put on their best clothes the following Saturday.

They piled into their red-and-white Chevrolet Impala, chattering away on the hour-long drive to Greensboro. Amari could hardly believe that she was going to make history. The line was long as many other black people also wanted to celebrate this civil rights milestone.

While she waited, Amari used her parents' camera to take pictures. She snapped the outside of Woolworth's first. Once she got inside, she took photos of the counter stools, the counter itself, and her meal. Amari was beaming from ear to ear as she savored every bite of her vanilla milkshake, hamburger, and French fries. No meal had ever tasted so good—or felt as celebratory—as that one.

Amari couldn't wait to write her next newspaper story with her first-hand account of eating in Greensboro. Maybe, just maybe, she'd get another article on the front page of the Battery Heights High School newspaper.

About the Civil Rights Movement

The Civil Rights Movement is a term used to describe the period of the 1950s and 1960s when there was a fight for racial equality in the United States. During this time, a number of leaders such as Dr. Martin Luther King Jr. and Rosa Parks led like-minded people to participate in non-violent protests. These protests came in many forms.

Throughout the southern states, there were laws that kept black people separate from white people. These laws were known as Jim Crow laws. Rosa Parks was arrested in 1955 for refusing to give up her seat on a bus to a white passenger. After Rosa Parks's arrest, a major protest took place. It was called the Montgomery Bus Boycott. For over a year, African-Americans boycotted public buses in Montgomery. On December 20, 1956, the Supreme Court ruled that bus segregation was illegal.

Sit-ins were another popular form of nonviolent protest during the Civil Rights Movement. Participants in sit-ins would enter a business or public place and remain seated until their grievances were addressed or they were forcibly removed. The Greensboro sit-in of 1960 was a successful nonviolent protest. The formerly segregated lunch counter in Woolworth's became open to all customers, black or white. The sit-in movement spread across the United States. It led to the desegregation of supermarkets, department stores, movie theaters, and libraries.

In July 1964, U.S. President Lyndon Johnson signed the Civil Rights Act into law. This outlawed segregation in all public places. It also outlawed discrimination against people based on their race, color, religion, sex, or national origin.

Q & A

with Alicia Klepeis

1. Where did you get the information for your book?

I started by reading several kids' books

on the Civil Rights Movement. I also used the Library of Congress website to gather images and information.

2. What was your process like for developing the main character?

I wanted Amari to be smart, energetic, and in touch with current events. But she is real, too. Amari gets bullied, fights with her parents, and eats too much candy.

3. Did you learn anything interesting while researching this era?

Tons. I didn't know much about the Greensboro sit-in. I loved researching the fashion, candy, and music of 1960 as well.

About the Author

Alicia Klepeis began her career at the National Geographic Society. She is the author of both fiction and nonfiction for young readers. Her fictional titles include *From Pizza to Pisa* and *Cairo, Camels, and Chaos*. Her nonfiction books include *The World's Strangest Foods, Bizarre Things We've Called Medicine,* and *Vampires: The Truth Behind History's Creepiest Bloodsuckers.* She lives with her family in upstate New York.

Websites to Visit

www.timeforkids.com/news/sitting-down-
    take-stand/5426
www.infoplease.com/spot/bhmheroes1.html
www.historyforkids.net/civil-rights.htm

Writing Prompt

Amari had to leave Boston and move to Raleigh in the middle of the school year. Have you ever been the new kid somewhere? How did your experience compare to Amari's?